Would You Be My friend?

LARRY D. D. CLIFFORD

Order this book online at www.trafford.com
or email orders@trafford.com

Most Trafford titles are also available at major online book retailers.

www.trafford.com

North America & international
toll-free: 844 688 6899 (USA & Canada)
fax: 812 355 4082

Our mission is to efficiently provide the world's finest, most comprehensive book publishing service, enabling every author to experience success. To find out how to publish your book, your way, and have it available worldwide, visit us online at www.trafford.com

ISBN: 978-1-6987-0721-1 (sc)
ISBN: 978-1-6987-0722-8 (e)

Print information available on the last page.

Trafford rev. 05/14/2021

Would You Be My friend?

By Larry D. D. Clifford
Illustrations by Tayler Corbisiero

In the lush green forest, there lived a Cougar named Clark. Clark was a very lonely cougar as no one would be his friend. Everyone was afraid of Clark because he looked and acted so much different than everyone else. So Clark decided to take a walk through the forest to see if he could find a friend.

Off Clark went to find a friend. Clark came upon a deer eating in the forest Clark said to the deer "I want to be your friend! Would you be my friend" The deer said, "You don't look like me. You have short legs and big teeth. You just don't fit in with my friends and me"!

And with one leap the deer
disappeared into the forest.

Clark came upon a Raccoon and he said to the raccoon, "Would you be my friend" The raccoon said to Clark, "How can we be friends? You don't look or act like a raccoon. You don't even have a mask. You don't wash your food before you eat it. We're just too different".

And off the raccoon
swam downstream.

As Clark was walking through the forest, he heard a noise in the tree. Clark looked up and saw an owl. Clark said to the owl, "Mr. Owl, my name is Clark and I want to know if you would be my friend"? The owl looked at Clark and said, "you don't have feathers, you can't fly, you talk funny and you can't even say ohooooooooo ohoooooooo.

And so off the
owl flew!

So sad Clark laid down on the ground, and just then, a little rabbit came hopping by. Clark said, "Hi Mr. Rabbit. What's your name"? The rabbit said "It's Jack, it's Jack Rabbit". Clark said to Jack, "I'm looking for a friend would you be my friend"? Jack said, "You don't know how to hop, you eat meat and all my friends eat grass".

And with one giant hop Jack disappeared into the forest! Clark was so sad and lonely he started walking through the forest with his head hung down.

Clark was sad because nobody liked him. "I don't fit in, I don't look like everyone else. I don't eat the same things they do, and I don't talk like everyone else". Just then, as Clark was walking through the forest with head hung low, a butterfly fluttered passed him. Clark was so sad he did not even notice the butterfly.

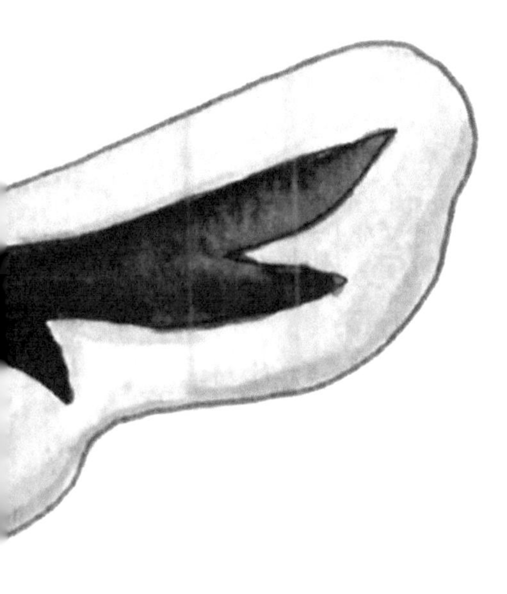

Then the butterfly turned around and flew back to Clark. The butterfly landed on Clark's nose. Clark was so amazed he could hardly talk!

Clark finally asked the butterfly, "What is your name"? The butterfly said, "My name is Donald"! Clark then said, "My name is Clark and nobody likes me. I can't hop, I don't look like them. I don't have a mask and I don't know how to fly"!

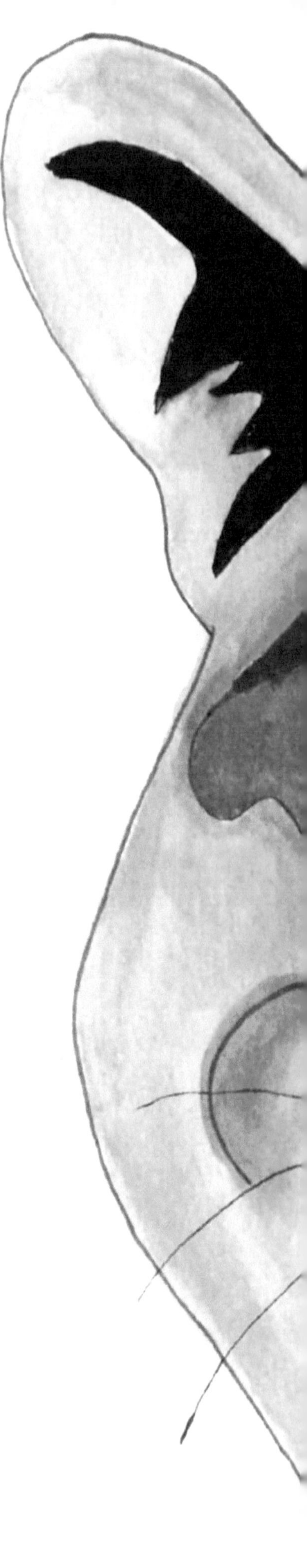

Donald said, "Just because we're different doesn't mean we can't be friends! And, so everywhere that Clark went, Donald the butterfly would ride on Clark's nose.

Just because Clark is tough doesn't mean he has to bully everyone to make friends. Clark and Donald were not alike but they had so much fun together because they were so different. They were always learning new things about each other.

The moral of the story... It does not matter who you are. Be honest and treat others with respect. Never stop looking for new friends. You will have good friend in your life forever!

Here is Clark and all his friends!

A few years ago I was asked to train a cougar for a zoo. The zoo wanted a feline exhibit area and needed to raise money for it. They wanted Clark to sit on a table and let people stand beside him and get their picture taken as a fund raiser.

They took me to the area where Clark was housed and I looked at Clark for a few minutes and could tell he was very lonely. The next day I started working with him. I simply sat outside his house feeding him small pieces of meat. I would also scratch him when he laid against the fence. After doing this for a few days I had a table put inside his house. When I went inside his house I would throw pieces of meat on the table getting him to jump on the table. After a few days, he knew when I went inside his house that's what I wanted him to do. I would walk around the table and feed him when was lying down.

Soon I had another trainer come inside Clark's house with me and stand beside him. We would take pictures of him so he got use to the noise of a camera. It was important that Clark get use to a lot of people around him. So I started to take him for walks in the park and hand him lay on the ground when people were around.

The big event came and Clark was one of the stars of the fund raiser. He was a very good boy sitting on the table letting people stand beside him and get their picture taken.

After the fund raiser was over, I only had a few days with Clark. When you train an animal for a show or program, you become friends and it's hard not to have them in your life, much like having a dog, cat or bird at home.

Clark will always be in my mind and heart, and miss him. I think he might even miss me.

- Larry Clifford

Larry and Clark taking a walk.

Pics from Larry's Scrapbook - Clark

Pics from Larry's Scrapbook

Larry with Ben the Bengal Tiger, Dolphin Riding at Sea World, and atop Shamu

Printed in the United States
by Baker & Taylor Publisher Services